Danny Dudley
Does the Dipsy Do

LUCIDBOOKS

Written by Jim Somerville

Illustrated by Andrew Laitinen

Danny Dudley Does the Dipsy Do

Published by Lucid Books in Houston, TX
www.lucidbookspublishing.com

eISBN: 978-1-63296-442-7
PB ISBN: 978-1-63296-440-3
HB ISBN: 978-1-63296-441-0

Special Sales: Most Lucid Books titles are available in special quantity discounts. Custom imprinting or excerpting can also be done to fit special needs. For standard bulk orders, go to www.lucidbooksbulk.com. For specialty press or large orders, contact Lucid Books at books@lucidbookspublishing.com.

To Kristine, for her encouragement and support

and

To all the little guys out there

Danny Dudley was a very smallish guy.
Next to the rest, he was barely chest high.
Even so, he was playing football this year
Because he wanted to conquer his fear.

The first day of practice they handed out pads,
So he got in line with the rest of the lads.
When Danny stepped up to take his turn,
The coach rubbed his chin with a look of concern.

"I don't know, Son, you're not very tall.
I don't think I have equipment that small."
He dug way down deep into the pile.
It actually took quite a little while.

Shoulder pads, knee pads, thigh pads, and girdle,
Finding them proved to be quite a hurdle.
The helmet they found, it scarcely fit,
But now Danny Dudley was ready to hit.

The coach didn't know where to have Danny play,
So Danny stood on the side for most of the day.
Coach thought, "Maybe safety or the lonely end.
He's just so small, it will have to depend."

At practice Danny played every here and there,
But Danny didn't really play anywhere.
The thing that all of them actually feared
Was playing in games would get Danny smeared.

The games came and went, one, two, three, and four.
Danny sat the bench, but he wasn't sore.
He thought, "Soon I'll get my chance to play.
I know I'll get in one of these days."

The last game of the year was on Labor Day,
And it caused the coach a great deal of dismay.
Dawkins was out of town, and Caldwell was ill,
Along with Carpenter, Walters, and Bob Rudesill.

The coach checked the count. "I'm one player short."
His face turned beet red and began to contort.
The assistant coach said, "Hey, we're okay.
We just have to let Danny Dudley play."

Danny Dudley finally got his chance
And began warming up in his three-point stance.
The coach thought, "Where will I have Dudley play?"
He prayed Danny would just stay out of the way.

So Danny lined up at the lonely end
The defense didn't bother to defend.
It was 11 on 10 most of the day,
But Danny was just happy he got to play.

The game was tied deep into the fourth.
Danny's team had the ball, they needed to score.
The handoff was made, and Danny hit the fray,
Though he was supposed to stay out of the way.

The back hit the hole but bounced it outside.
He and the tackler were about to collide.
The back caught his cleat and began to stumble.
Then the hit was made, and out popped the fumble!

The ball hit the turf then popped into the air.
Lo and behold, Danny Dudley was there.
Coach's eyes got big as he looked in alarm.
The ball landed squarely in Danny's arms.

The back on the ground yelled to Danny, "Run!"
So Danny took off and thought, "Boy, is this fun!"
He ran to the left and then to the right.
Three tacklers bore down with all of their might.

Danny saw them coming from all around,
And when they all converged, he left the ground.
Danny twisted and spun and flew through the air.
The tacklers collided, but he wasn't there.

He landed legs churning toward the goalpost,
Reincarnating the Galloping Ghost.
The crowd was cheering a deafening sound.
Danny Dudley just scored the winning touchdown!

His teammates ran screaming to the end zone.
"That's the greatest move we've ever been shown!"
It was the grandest move in gridiron lore,
A move no one had ever seen before.

"How you did that move I don't have a clue."
Danny said, "Why, Coach, that's my 'dipsy do'!
I twist and spin and fly through the air,
I land on my feet, and then I'm not there."

Pondering how just gets your thoughts muddled.
Trying to explain gets your brain all befuddled.
And that day to this no one ever knew
How Danny Dudley did his dipsy do.

Jim Somerville was born in Romulus, a small town in upstate New York, and currently resides in Watkins Glen, New York. He and his wife, Kristine, have three children. Jim attended Romulus Central School and then went on to receive a bachelor's degree in sports medicine from Messiah College. Growing up, he played almost every sport and was one of the "smallish guys" until late in high school. During his 20-year career as a certified athletic trainer, Jim has worked with dozens of sports and thousands of athletes in high schools, colleges, and clinical settings.

CPSIA information can be obtained
at www.ICGtesting.com
Printed in the USA
BVHW021431060421
604326BV00007B/446